The Five Outer Chakras
and
the Etheric Web

Patsy Stanley

PB ISBN 9798993585673

The Five Outer Chakras and the Etheric Web is a gentle but powerful introduction to the hidden structures that surround and sustain human life. Beyond the seven familiar chakras lies a set of **five outer energy centers**—subtle, luminous points that form a bridge between the personal self and the vast cosmos we are woven into. These outer chakras anchor intuition, purpose, ancestral memory, soul-level direction, and the quiet wisdom that whispers to us from the higher realms. Within and between these centers stretches the **etheric web**, a living lattice of light. It is both map and messenger—transmitting impressions, guiding our evolution, and revealing how deeply connected we are to the rhythms of the universe. Understanding this web allows us to recognize the similarities threading through all forms of life...

the repeating patterns, the cycles, the echoes that remind us that nothing stands alone. This little book offers a clear pathway for readers who feel ready to learn higher things. With simplicity and depth, it explains how the outer chakras function, why they awaken, and how recognizing them can open the door to a more meaningful, aligned, and luminous existence. Step into a wider understanding of who you are—and the universe you are part of.

Most metaphysical teachings tell us we have seven major chakras throughout our bodies. Some studies list both minor and major chakras and elsewhere.

We also have chakras outside of our bodies that are connected to us. Those chakras constantly connect and remind our individual life force what the universe means to us, and reminds us that we are a part of the universe, and are connected to it at all times. Those chakras define our place in the larger scheme of Life. We live and die just as the stars in the cosmos do. To track the birth and magnificent death of a star, is to track our own beginning and endings.

We are birthed and live and fade and die, just as stars do. We are a particle of Light-motion and Matter connected to and moving within a larger universe. Everything we know about is participating in the larger universal laws.

Our connection to All of Life is maintained through the vital Cosmic energies, the collection of Universal,

Galactic

Galactic Super cluster,

Solar system,

Sun,

And Planetary

Energies that run through the personal chakra system connected to the Etheric web located outside of our bodies.

We must be fed these energies in order to maintain to exist- to continue being a part of the Cosmos. This is the Larger Law that rules All. These energy exchanges in all their complexities take place through what we call the chakra system.

However, it doesn't stop there. We not only agree to the two Birth and Death initiations on planet Earth, we agree to help Earth with its own energy processes and growth. Since we're made of the same star material Earth is made of, we can do this.

Depending on when we show up here and how, we agree to join soul groups that are processing Earth energies-as well as our own- at that time.

We live and die in soul groups. We have to participate in Earths life events. Earth is a huge living being that we live on. And Earth, like other planets out there, has its ups and downs. It has different ages and cycles it lives through. Earth may become too wet or too dry. Too hot or cold. And, there are the bigger events Earth lives through, like the elliptical issues that arise approximately every 13,000 years when it turns the corner, and we have to help it shift its polarity to the opposite one it has been in. That's matriarchy-patriarchy stuff.

It has been written in esoteric literature that the Earth has been cleansed of human beings and the life forms surrounding them and re-seeded at least ten times.

So humans go through scourges and ravages, plagues, and pandemics and still want to come back here to planet Earth. It is a beautiful, terrifying classroom of life, a rugged and monstrous and the best ever classroom to learn lessons in.

The Outer Chakras:

Most metaphysical teachings tell us we have seven major chakras throughout our bodies. Some teachings/studies list both minor and major chakras here and there and elsewhere, changing the numbers and placements to match the cultural system using it.

Whatever number you decide on, we also have at least five chakras outside of the crown chakra-head- spinning faster than any of our internalized human chakras.

Who knows exactly how many chakras connect us by law to the Universe, the Cosmos and to whatever else is out there? By Law, we have to be connected. Because we are made of star material- the same thing everything else is made of.

The number and kind of outer chakras most likely vary, depending on where we manifested at birth, our cause for being here, (causal bodies), cultures, and many other factors. For our purpose, we are talking about the five outer chakras that spin outside the head.

They circle your head about eighteen inches out, and spin. The crown chakra at the top of your head picks up the five outer crown chakra energies after they are processed through your Etheric web which surrounds your physical body. Then they are transmuted utilizing your ancestral transmuting genetic/systems. That processing includes our ancient genetics, which code purpose and intention. Then they are poured down into our system. Remember that down equals slower. Up equals faster.

The outer chakras constantly connect and remind our individual life force that we have a place in the Universe. This balancing act keeps us in constant expansion-evolution- and is the constantly unfolding purpose behind what we call Evolution.

The five outer chakras connect us to the energies of the larger life of the Universe, the Cosmos, and to the Greater Mysteries.

The five outer chakras keep us connected to the larger life we are a part of at all times. We came from the cosmos. We are made of its materials. Whether we like it or not, it doesn't change that it is true.

The five outer chakras define our place in the larger scheme of Life.

We are birthed and live and begin to fade and die, just as stars do. We are connected to the stars. The Universe. We are made of Star material.

Each piece of life on Earth must follow the laws governing our passage on Earth. People, plants, minerals, etc. All of it.

We are a tiny part of life following the laws that connect the parts moving within each larger universe to each other.

Our connection to All of Life is maintained through the vital Cosmic energies we receive through these cosmic outer chakras.

Universal

Galactic-Galactic Super cluster

Solar system

Sun

Planetary-Inner body

Not only are humans connected to the universe through these outer chakras, so is everything else. Plants. Animals. Rocks. You name it. No one is exempt. Nothing is exempt. We as a part of the Earth's species have those connections and their input in common. It is one of the ways that allows us to be spiritually alike. To enable souls to dwell within each and everything there is.

Each cosmic charka has energy meridians that feed/carry its chakra energies to the Etheric web. All energy meridians are connected to and meet at the Etheric web located outside of our four basic bodies.

At that point, a conversion process takes place. The cosmic energies are slowed down so they can be processed for use by our personal energy systems. The calibrated energies are then sent from the Etheric web to our inner chakra system to be processed again.

This process takes place through our external chakra and meridian system. The Cosmic collection of these energies is fed to our Etheric web through the outer chakras that gravitate outside of and around our physical head and bodies. We can't see them, but they are there. They are spinning so fast that we can't see them.

The five cosmic chakras are energetically aligned with the ridges in the upper occipital lobe of the physical body's head. Their meridians are attached at specific areas of service to the Etheric body.

The five cosmic chakras are attached through meridians to the causal bodies of each part of everything that has manifested on this planet. That includes human beings.

The Etheric body works with the Ether Element. It looks like a moving, flexible grid. It is a net or web surrounding ourselves. No one knows exactly how far it stands out from each of our four our bodies, but we can guess that it is fluid, flexible, and at places, within a few inches of our physical body.

The vibration of the Etheric web resonates to the Etheric grids surrounding Earth, and it is a match for them. Therefore, causing healing to our bodies to be available through the Colors and Elements that comprise Earth.

We can speculate that the magnetic energy grids surrounding Earth are Earth's Etheric energy web.

Each of our Cosmic or outer energy chakras is attached to through meridian paths and works with a different part of our Etheric body, the energy body, the web or net, that surrounds us.

All the outer chakras spin at a higher vibration, and this is why. The Etheric body resides outside of the self, the bodies our other chakras are encased in. The result is that it has very little matter it is attached to. That attachment would normally slow the spin down. It is fluidic and delicate as a result, but extremely strong. It is the gateway between the inner and outer realms of form.

These energies flood the causal bodies- the spiritual energy fields between each of the four body forms-as well as the Etheric field.

When the Etheric body is rent or torn or damaged in some way, it takes spiritual energy to get to it and do the work to heal it. You can't get there to heal it or even work on it, until the energy is high enough in vibration. This is why rituals and spiritual ceremonies have to be the tools used to pave the way to Etheric body healing. Those things raise the vibration. This holds true for your other bodies, too. That is the basis for enlightenment energies and their many forms and rituals.

We are perfectly put together. We are a finely organized machine

The active tools of Imagination must be used, because those tools allow us to explore things not presently in our physical environment or world. The tools of the Imagination are used in a whole variety of cognitive processes including planning, hypothetical reasoning, picturing things in the past or future, design, creativity, and understanding language. Matter cannot be brought into the realms of Outer Form without using the tools of the Imagination. There is a whole tool box in there. Check it out.

Think of the Etheric Web as a web or a grid, with crossing points allowing you entrance into new worlds. At each quarter inch apart, sits a crossing point. At this crossing point is seated a spinning sphere containing and maintaining a small amount of the perfect, most delicately tuned, chemical mix of colors and elements, calibrated for only you, that came from the universe birthing a star somewhere billions of years ago. Mind boggling perfection!

These tiny, delicate, perfectly and personally balanced spheres constantly feed measured doses of Cosmic energies constantly timed, to each particle of us, so that we are maintained in the deeper realms of understanding located in the Greater Forces we are a part of.

After the Etheric web sorts out these energies, the energies are delivered down into our soul planes of energy and sorted again. This refining process receives the data from these chakras and sorts with one foundation in mind. That is, to help us recognize the similarities all things have to one another. This process of understanding takes place on the soul planes very slowly in terms of human time.

The five outer chakras connect us to our Cosmic Elders who reside in the Great Cosmic Seas, Skies, and many other places.

We have a built in tracker so the Universe knows where we are at all times. Under the third eye sits a hologram of the planet Earth. It is located at the top of the bridge of the nose in human beings. This seats the third eye into Earth's dimensions, and grounds it there.

The hologram of Earth we carry is the identity map that allows the cosmic chakras to attach to and work with the Earth's own dimensions. This hologram also identifies us as to where we are located in the universe. Yes, the universe has us on GPS!

The cosmic chakras are connected to the upper occipital ridge in the head, and from there, their energies are transported faster than the speed of light, which means other time dimensions, into portals running from your cranial plates and out to about 18 inches around your face, like a mask of energy.

Your sense of smell and sight-check out their location-is faster than any of your other senses. These are the senses that regulate the speed of, and send these energies into the proper places in the rest of your systems.

We stay connected to the cosmos through the intervention of these outer chakras. The Universe is 13.8 billion years old. The Earth is 4 and a half billion years old.

Studying the universe out there is a way is to learn about the Macrocosm. Our outer chakras spin faster than the seven internal body chakras. Those chakras reflect the inner Nature of all things. To study the inner workings of anything is to study the microcosm.

The outer chakras reside outside of the physical body because they have a higher and more expanded vibration. The outer chakras spin faster than any of our other chakras, emitting more of their energies, so expansion is provided, by the universe wisely placing ours outside but attached to the self.

They are the necessary linkage maintaining the connections between us and the universal energies which we are made of. The outer chakras embody and maintain for each of us, the Law that All Life lives by, so that All can continue to exist, and never die, just change form time after time. In understanding this principle, we realize our greatest form of immortality.

Our outer chakras are faster moving than our physical, mental, astral, and soul body chakras. What that means is, we have a permanent connection to the Cosmos that lasts after we transcend our physical bodies.

To study the Cosmos is to learn how higher beginnings and endings happen and how true separation and true connection works. This study allows further membership into the larger understanding of the higher, collective, spiritual Nature of Life. From this, we understand more of how we are alike.

This kind of work helps the opening of the higher inner chakras.

We are truly Star material...

Every Master that is your teacher is a strand of your Cosmic DNA.

At this time, the outer chakras are being activated in all beings populating planet Earth, including humans, because those connections are needed to help the planet we live on to make changes. Planet Earth is a living being that processes change much as humans process change.

Planet Earth uses different time frames than human beings, plants, or animals do. Planet Earth's time frames are much longer than human beings time frames. We are tiny.

It doesn't take us as much time to change as does a larger body. So we won't be around to see much of the stuff that changes. Our generations might.

Earth doesn't travel in a perfect circle. It's path is elliptical. It is predictable that every time the Earth rounds the outer turn, that it will change big time. We get to see some of that-what a ride!

So don't stay small –the changes will go on no matter what you believe, feel, think. Or try to do. Best to go with the flow. After all this is a classroom where you are a student learning about life.

This is a very big process and lots of planets and energies are participating to change the energy vibrations of many things. There is a shaking out process in which people and plants and animals and others are leaving Planet Earth. Who knows where they go? We do know they live on. Because energy never dies, it just changes form time after time.

Yes. You chose to be here now. All souls choose the groups they belong to, and will act with before they can manifest here. That is required. It a Covenant agreed to by this planet and you. Before the earth gifts you with a body, and all your issues to learn from, you have to make a Covenant about how you will participate on Planet Earth with the planetary energies.

You support the Earths growth or you wouldn't be allowed here.

And Earth supports your growth. You can't change your mind or back out either on the agreement, though many have tried. You might as well face the fact that your soul chose this time to be here, and let it get on with its job.

The Cosmic collection of these energies, and possibly more, are fed to our Etheric web through the outer chakras that gravitate outside of, and around our head and bodies.

These chakras are energetically aligned with the ridges in the upper occipital lobe of the head, and are attached at strategic areas to the Etheric body, and to the causal bodies of each part of manifested collective matter on this planet. That includes human beings.

The Etheric body works with the Ether Element. It looks like a net or web surrounding ourselves. No one knows exactly how far out it is from our bodies, but we can estimate that it is fluid, flexible, and at places, within a few inches of our physical body.

The vibration of the Etheric web resonates to the grids surrounding Earth and is a match for them, therefore causing healing to our bodies to be available through the Colors and Elements that comprise Earth.

The magnetic energy grids surrounding Earth is its Etheric web and connect the Earth to its outer chakras and the cosmos.

Each one of the Cosmic energy chakras works with a different part of the Etheric body, the energy body the web or net that surrounds us.

The outer chakras spin at a higher vibration, and this is why. The Etheric body resides outside of the physical self of anything, so it has very little matter to slow the spin down. It is fluidic and delicate as a result, but extremely strong.

When the Etheric body is rent or torn or damaged in some way, it takes what we call spiritual energy to get to it and do the work to heal it. You can't get there to heal it or even work on it, until the energy is raised high enough in vibration.

Rituals and ceremonies raises the energies of the energy-tools used to access the Etheric body to heal it. You have to match the higher energies.

Think of the Etheric Web as a web or a grid, with crossing points. At each crossing point is seated a spinning sphere containing and maintaining a small amount of the perfect, most delicately tuned, chemical mix of colors and elements just suited for you, that came from the universe birthing a star somewhere a long time ago. Billions of years ago.

These delicate, perfectly and personally balanced chakra systems, feed constantly measured doses of the Cosmic energies to each particle of us, so that we are maintained in the deeper understanding of the Greater Forces we are a tiny part of. These chakras connect us to our Cosmic Elders who reside in the Great Cosmic Seas, and elsewhere.

We have a built in tracker so the universe knows where we are at all times. Under the third eye sits a hologram of the Earth at the bridge of the nose in human beings. This seats the third eye into Earth's dimensions and grounds it there.

It is our identity map that allows the cosmic chakras to attach to, and work with the Earth dimensions. Our physical body. This hologram also identifies us as to where we are located in this universe.

The cosmic chakras are connected to the upper occipital ridge in the head, and from there, their energies are transported faster than the speed of light, which means other time dimensions, into portals running from your cranial plates and out to about eighteen inches from your head, like a mask of energy.

Your sense of smell and sight are faster than any of your other senses. These are the senses that regulate the speed of, and send these energies into the rest of the system.

We stay connected to the cosmos through the intervention of these outer chakras. The Universe is 13.8 billion years old. The Earth is 4 and a half billion years old.

These chakras spin faster than the seven physical body chakras. That is why they reside outside of the physical body. They have to reside outside of the body because of their higher vibration. They spin faster, in order to maintain the linkage between us and the universal energies. These chakras embody and maintain for each of us, the Law that All Life lives by, so that All can continue to exist.

These chakras are faster moving than our physical, mental, astral, and soul bodies. That means that we have a permanent connection to the cosmos that lasts after we transcend our physical bodies.

To study the Cosmos is to learn how higher beginnings and endings happen and how true separation and true connection works. This study allows further membership into the larger understanding of the higher, collective, spiritual Nature of Life. From this, we understand more of how we are alike.

This kind of work helps the opening of the higher inner chakras.

We are truly Star material...

We go through the same birth, aging and death process the stars go through. . We do this to refine and collect the best of ourselves for our next adventure in the cosmos, just as the stars do. Good traveling to you!

More metaphysical books by Patsy Stanley:

The Elements
The Spiritual Nature of Atomic Structure
Chakras, Meridians, and the Color Energies
The Mental Body
Sound Energies
Shield Energies
The Four Bodies

All of these metaphysical books are available through all online bookstores including Amazon and Barnes & Noble.